# THE CURSED PORTRAIT : A HAUNTING LOVE STORY

ANKIT VASHISHTA

Made with ♥ on the Notion Press Platform
www.notionpress.com

I dedicate this Book to the reader who is reading this.
Thank you for reading this book.

# Contents

# PREFACE

This is the story of Dr. Raj, a professor at a local university, who finds himself drawn into a dark mystery when he investigates a strange sighting in one of the dormitories. What begins as a simple investigation quickly spirals into a haunting tale of love and obsession, as Dr. Raj uncovers a sinister letter and a painting that seems to hold a mysterious power.

As he delves deeper into the mystery, Dr. Raj must confront his own fears and doubts, as well as the dangerous secrets that lie buried in the past. With the help of a few unlikely allies, he must uncover the truth about the girl in the painting, and the dark forces that threaten to consume them all.

In this gripping tale of horror and suspense, nothing is as it seems, and the past has a way of coming back to haunt us in the most unexpected ways. Prepare to be chilled to the bone as you journey into the dark heart of this unforgettable story.

As you read this book, you will be transported to a world that is both familiar and strange, where nothing is as it seems and danger lurks around every corner. The author hopes that this book will leave you on the edge of your seat, eagerly turning the pages to find out what happens next.

# PROLOGUE

It was my first day at one of the best medical colleges in India. I had always dreamed of becoming a doctor, and this college was my first step towards achieving that dream. As I walked through the corridors, I could feel the excitement building inside me. The college was vast and imposing, with a rich history that was evident in every nook and corner.

As I explored the college, I stumbled upon an old dormitory that looked abandoned and decrepit. A sense of curiosity overtook me, and I wondered why such a place was off-limits. I tried to push open the creaky door, but it was locked. I decided to leave it at that and continued exploring the rest of the college.

But the memory of the old dormitory lingered in my mind. As the days passed, I became more and more curious about what was inside. I asked my fellow students about it, but no one seemed to know anything about the dormitory. In fact, they seemed to actively avoid talking about it.

Untill I found Sheena, she was my Super Senior. She had thick curly hairs and was wearing big round glasses and a Baggy Pair of Jeans and a Boyfriend top. She told me that the old dormitory has long been shrouded in mystery and intrigue. For years, students have whispered about this abandoned dormitory and the strange happenings that occur within its walls. People told that this dormitory was once home to a group of students who dabbled in the dark arts. They were said to have summoned spirits and demons, conducting rituals that were both forbidden and dangerous.

She added that Those who dare to venture inside the dormitory are met with a feeling of unease and foreboding.

The air is thick with a sense of malevolence, and the darkness seems to seep into your very bones. Some have even heard the sounds of disembodied voices whispering in their ears, promising secrets and power beyond their wildest dreams.

One night, I couldn't resist my curiosity any longer. I snuck out of my dorm room and made my way to the old dormitory. The door was still locked, but I managed to find a way in through a broken window. The dormitory was dark and eerie, with an unsettling feeling that I couldn't quite shake off.

As I walked through the dusty corridors, I noticed a faint light coming from the end of the hallway. Intrigued, I followed it and found myself at a small wooden door. Without hesitation, I opened the door and found myself in a dimly lit room with an old bookcase and a table. There was a pathway leading out of the room, and I felt drawn to follow it.

As I walked down the pathway, I emerged into a dense forest. The air was thick with the scent of pine, and I could hear the rustling of leaves and twigs under my feet. The trees seem to reach up to the sky like twisted fingers, their branches creaking and swaying in the wind like bony arms. As I ventured deeper into the forest, the trees seem to close in around me, creating a feeling of claustrophobia and isolation. The rustling of leaves and snapping of twigs underfoot sound like whispers and footsteps, making me feel like I was being followed by an unseen presence.

The air is thick with the scent of decay and dampness, as though the forest is rotting from within. It's easy to imagine that the trees themselves are alive, their twisted and gnarled trunks and branches forming grotesque faces and shapes.

Suddenly, a woman appeared in front of me. She was tall and striking, with long flowing hair and piercing eyes. She wore a flowing white gown, and there was an aura of power and wisdom emanating from her.

"Who are you?" I asked, my heart racing.

"I am the Second Sister," she replied, her voice calm and soothing. "I have been waiting for you."

I was taken aback. "Waiting for me? Why?" "I have been watching you, young one," she said, "and I see great potential in you. Potential for healing, for wisdom, for knowledge. But you must be careful.

There are forces in this world that seek to corrupt and destroy. You must be strong and vigilant if you are to succeed."

I listened to her words, feeling both humbled and inspired. As she spoke, I felt a sense of clarity and purpose growing inside me.

"And remember," the Second Sister said, "you are never truly alone. There are always those who will guide and protect you, even in the darkest of times. Just like Dr. Raj did for Shreya"

"Dr. Raj? You mean Dr. Raj, Head of Department Neurology?" I asked curiously.

Yes!. She said. Let me tell you a story about a mysterious painting, that changed the life of a Dr. Raj to a responsible, loving, caring and a forgiving doctor.

# I

# Uncovering the Mystery of the Haunted Painting

Dr. Raj had never been one for staying up late. As a professor at the local university, he had a strict routine that he adhered to in order to maintain his focus and productivity during the day. But tonight was different. As he made his way down the dimly-lit corridor of the dormitory, he felt a sense of restlessness that he couldn't shake.

It was well past midnight, and the building was silent except for the soft hum of the air conditioning units. Dr. Raj had been asked to visit the dormitory by one of his students, who had reported seeing something strange in one of the rooms. He wasn't sure what to expect, but he knew that he had to investigate.

As he walked past the rows of doors, he noticed that one of them was slightly ajar. He hesitated for a moment before pushing it open, not wanting to invade anyone's privacy.

But as he stepped inside, he saw that the room was empty, except for a small painting hanging on the wall.

It was a portrait of a young woman with dark hair and piercing blue eyes. She was wearing a flowing white dress, and her expression was both serene and melancholy. Dr. Raj couldn't help but be drawn to the painting. It was both beautiful and haunting, and he found himself wondering who the girl in the portrait was.

As he examined the painting more closely, he noticed that there was something written in the corner in small, elegant script. He leaned in to read it, and his heart skipped a beat as he saw what it said:

"To my dearest Shreya, may this painting remind you of our love forever."

Dr. Raj felt a chill run down his spine as he realized that he had stumbled upon something much more sinister than a simple painting. He couldn't help but wonder who Lily was, and what had happened to her. And as he looked around the empty dorm room, he knew that he had to find out the truth.

Dr. Raj stared at the portrait of the girl, Shreya, with a mixture of curiosity and unease. He couldn't help but wonder what the story was behind this haunting painting, and the letter attached to it only piqued his interest further.

He reached out and carefully detached the envelope from the back of the frame. It was yellowed with age and sealed with a wax stamp that had long since cracked and faded. Dr. Raj's heart raced as he carefully opened the envelope, feeling as though he was about to uncover a long-kept secret.

Inside the envelope, there was a letter written in an elegant hand. Dr. Raj recognized the style of writing from the script on the painting. It read:

*"My dearest Shreya,*

*I hope this painting finds you well. I know that we are separated by many miles, but I feel as though you are here with me whenever I look at it. You are the light of my life, my reason for being. I cannot wait until the day when we can be together again, free from the constraints of this cruel world.*

*I know that our love is unconventional, and that there are those who would judge us harshly for it. But I do not care. I would do anything for you, Shreya. I would cross oceans, climb mountains, and face any challenge that comes our way.*

*I know that you have doubts sometimes, that you wonder if we are doing the right thing. But trust me when I say that our love is worth any sacrifice. We are meant to be together, now and forever.*

*Yours always,*

*Vikram"*

Dr. Raj felt a chill run down his spine as he read the letter. There was something deeply unsettling about the tone of it, the sense of possession and control that Vikram seemed to exert over Shreya. He couldn't help but wonder what kind of relationship the two of them had, and what had happened to Shreya.

He examined the painting again, looking for any clues as to Shreya's identity or whereabouts. But there was nothing on the canvas that could tell him anything more than what the letter had revealed.

As he stood there in the silent dorm room, Dr. Raj knew that he couldn't leave this mystery unsolved. He had to find out who Shreya was, and what had happened to her. And he was willing to go to any lengths to do so.

Dr. Raj sat at his desk, the painting of Shreya propped up on the surface in front of him. He had been researching for hours, scouring the internet and pouring over old records in an effort to uncover the truth behind the mysterious letter he had found.

He had managed to piece together a few facts about Vikram, the author of the letter. He had been a student at the university many years ago, and had been involved in a number of controversial incidents during his time there. But there was little information about Shreya herself, no records or news articles that could shed light on who she was or what had happened to her.

Dr. Raj rubbed his eyes, feeling the fatigue beginning to set in. He knew that he needed to rest, to clear his head and approach the problem with fresh eyes in the morning. But something about the painting and the letter had captured his imagination, and he couldn't bear the thought of leaving it unresolved.

As he sat there, lost in thought, his phone rang. He answered it absentmindedly, not expecting anyone to be calling him at this hour.

"Hello?" he said.

"Dr. Raj?" the voice on the other end was urgent, breathless. "You have to help me. It's about the painting."

Dr. Raj sat up straight, his heart racing. "Who is this?"

"It doesn't matter. You have to come to the dormitory right away. Room 207. Please, hurry."

The line went dead, leaving Dr. Raj with a sense of foreboding. He stood up, grabbing his coat and the painting, and rushed out of his office. He couldn't shake the feeling that he was walking into something dangerous, but he knew that he had to see it through.

As he made his way through the deserted campus, he couldn't help but wonder who had called him and what they wanted. Were they involved in the mystery of the painting and the letter? Or was it just a coincidence?

When he arrived at the dormitory, he found the door to room 207 ajar, just as it had been the night before. He pushed it open cautiously, stepping inside.

The room was in disarray, with overturned furniture and scattered belongings strewn across the floor. Dr. Raj felt a knot form in his stomach. He knew that he had stumbled onto something dangerous, something that could put him in harm's way. But he couldn't back down now. He had to find out what was going on, and he had to do it fast.

He bent down to examine the room, hoping to salvage some clue. As he started searching at that dark scary dormitory 207 he found a small metal box nestled inside. He opened it with shaking hands, revealing a collection of old photographs, newspaper clippings, and handwritten notes.

As he scanned the contents of the box, Dr. Raj felt a chill run down his spine. There was more to this mystery than he had ever imagined. And he knew that the answers were waiting for him.

# II

# The Warning

Dr. Raj sifted through the contents of the metal box, his mind racing as he tried to make sense of the pieces of the puzzle that were slowly falling into place. The photographs were old and faded, depicting scenes from the university many years ago. He recognized some of the buildings, the landmarks that had been there for decades.

But it was the handwritten notes that caught his attention. They were written in an elegant script, the ink faded with time. As he read through them, he noticed that many of them contained Sanskrit shlokas, ancient verses that spoke of power and magic.

Dr. Raj felt a shiver run down his spine as he read through the verses. He had always been fascinated by the occult, the idea that there were forces beyond the rational, measurable world. But he had never believed that he would be confronted with it so directly.

As he continued to read, he began to feel a strange energy in the room. It was as if the shlokas were alive, resonating with a power that he could not comprehend. He closed his eyes, focusing on the feeling, trying to understand it.

Suddenly, he felt a hand on his shoulder. He jumped, startled, and spun around to face the intruder.

It was a young woman, her face obscured by the shadows of the room. "Who are you?" he demanded.

The woman didn't answer, instead reaching out and taking the box from his hands. She opened it, scanning the contents with a practiced eye.

"You shouldn't be here," she said finally. "This is not your place."

Dr. Raj bristled at her tone. "I have as much right to be here as anyone else. And I have a feeling that you know more about this than you're letting on."

The woman looked at him, her eyes piercing. "You are playing with fire, Dr. Raj. The forces you are meddling with are not to be trifled with. You would do well to leave this alone."

Dr. Raj felt a surge of anger at her condescending tone. He had always been his own person, unafraid to take risks and pursue his own path. He wasn't about to back down now.

"I will not be intimidated by you," he said firmly. "I have a feeling that there is more to this mystery than anyone realizes. And I intend to find out what it is."

The woman regarded him for a long moment, her eyes inscrutable. Finally, she nodded. "Very well. But be warned. The path you are on is fraught with danger. And there are forces at work here that are beyond your understanding."

With that, she turned and left the room, disappearing into the shadows.

Dr. Raj sat there for a long time, feeling the weight of her words sinking in. He knew that he was on the cusp of something extraordinary, something that could change his life forever. But he also knew that there were risks involved, risks that he couldn't fully comprehend.

As he gathered the contents of the box and prepared to leave the dormitory, he couldn't help but wonder what lay ahead. And whether he was ready for the journey that lay before him.

Dr. Raj stepped out of the dormitory, the cool night air hitting him like a wave. He looked up at the stars, feeling a sense of wonder and awe wash over him. There was so much he didn't know about the world, so much that lay beyond the boundaries of his understanding.

He walked down the path, lost in thought, replaying the events of the evening over and over in his mind. He was so deep in thought that he almost didn't notice the figure standing in front of him until it was too late.

He stumbled, barely managing to catch himself before he fell. "What the..." he began, looking up at the figure.

It was the woman from the dormitory, her features illuminated by the soft glow of the streetlight. "I'm sorry to startle you," she said. "But I couldn't let you leave without speaking to you again."

Dr. Raj bristled, feeling a sense of annoyance wash over him. "What more could you possibly have to say to me?" he demanded.

The woman regarded him coolly. "Just this. Be careful. The painting you found is more than just a piece of art. It is a window into something much deeper, much more mysterious than you can imagine."

Dr. Raj felt a shiver run down his spine at her words. "What are you saying?" he asked.

The woman shook her head, her eyes inscrutable. "I cannot say more. But I urge you to be cautious. There are forces at work here that are beyond your understanding."

With that, she turned and walked away, disappearing into the darkness.

Dr. Raj stood there for a long time, feeling the weight of her words sinking in. He knew that he had stumbled onto something big, something that could change his life forever. But he also knew that there were risks involved, risks that he couldn't fully comprehend.

As he walked back to his car, he couldn't help but wonder what lay ahead. And whether he was ready for the journey that lay before him. The mysteries of the painting and the shlokas echoed in his mind, their meaning still shrouded in shadow. But one thing was clear. He was not alone in his quest. And the woman who had warned him was watching, waiting for him to make his next move.

The next morning, Dr. Raj woke up with a sense of determination. He had spent the night thinking about the woman's warning, and he knew that he couldn't simply ignore it. He needed to learn more about the painting and the shlokas, and he needed to do it quickly.

After a quick breakfast, he drove to the local library, his mind already racing with questions. As he entered the building, he was greeted by the smell of old books and the sound of rustling pages.

He headed straight to the section on Indian art and culture, scanning the shelves for anything that might be useful. After a few minutes, he found a book on Indian mythology and spirituality, written by a renowned scholar of Sanskrit.

He flipped through the pages, his eyes scanning the dense text for any mention of the shlokas he had heard the night before. And then, he saw it. A passage about a mysterious painting that was said to hold great power, a painting that was believed to be a portal to another realm.

Dr. Raj's heart began to race as he read on. The painting was said to be guarded by powerful spirits, and only those with a pure heart and a strong will could hope to unlock its secrets.

He closed the book, his mind whirring with possibilities. Was the painting he had found the same one described in the book? And if so, what did it mean for him? Was he the one with the pure heart and the strong will?

As he left the library, he couldn't help but feel a sense of excitement mingled with fear. He was entering a world that was far beyond his understanding, a world of ancient magic and secret knowledge. But he knew that he had to go forward, that he had to find out what lay at the heart of the mystery.

And so, he resolved to return to the dormitory that night, to study the painting and the shlokas in more detail. He knew that it was risky, that he was playing with forces that he could not fully control. But he also knew that he had come too far to turn back now.

As the sun began to set, Dr. Raj found himself standing once again in front of the dormitory. He took a deep breath, feeling a sense of anticipation building inside him. Whatever lay ahead, he was ready to face it.

# III

# The Search for the Secrets of the Painting and the Shlokas

Dr. Raj entered the dormitory, his eyes scanning the walls for any sign of the mysterious woman who had warned him the night before. But there was no trace of her. The hallways were empty, the rooms dark and silent.

He made his way to the room where he had found the painting, the shlokas echoing in his mind. He stood there for a long time, studying the painting in silence. The girl in the painting seemed to be staring back at him, her eyes filled with a sense of longing and sadness.

As he studied the painting, he felt a sense of unease creeping over him. He knew that he was treading on dangerous ground, that he was playing with forces that he could not fully comprehend. But he also knew that he had to keep going, that he had to unravel the mystery of the painting and the shlokas.

And then, as if on cue, he heard a sound behind him. He turned around, his heart racing, and saw the woman standing in the doorway.

She regarded him coolly, her eyes flickering with a mixture of curiosity and suspicion. "What are you doing here?" she demanded.

Dr. Raj stepped forward, his eyes fixed on hers. "I need your help," he said. "I need to know more about the painting and the shlokas."

The woman's expression softened slightly. "Why should I help you?" she asked.

Dr. Raj took a deep breath, feeling a sense of desperation building inside him. "Because I think you know more than you're letting on," he said. "I think you have the key to unlocking the mystery, and I need your help to do it."

The woman regarded him for a long moment, her eyes searching his face for any sign of deception. And then, slowly, she nodded.

"Very well," she said. "But you must understand that this is dangerous territory. The painting and the shlokas are not to be taken lightly. They hold a power that can be both good and evil, depending on how they are used."

Dr. Raj nodded, feeling a sense of relief wash over him. He knew that he was taking a risk, but he also knew that he had no other choice.

And so, with the woman's guidance, he began his search for the secrets of the painting and the shlokas. Together, they studied ancient texts and explored hidden corners of the city, seeking out clues and piecing together the fragments of a mystery that had been hidden for centuries.

As they delved deeper into the world of ancient magic and occult knowledge, Dr. Raj felt himself becoming more and more obsessed with the painting and the shlokas. He knew that he was taking a risk, that he was playing with fire. But he also knew that he could not stop, that he had to keep going, no matter what the cost.

Days turned into weeks, and Dr. Raj's search for the secrets of the painting and the shlokas continued. His meetings with the mysterious woman became more frequent, and their discussions grew more intense.

He spent countless hours studying ancient Sanskrit texts and exploring the hidden corners of the city, seeking out any clue that could help him unravel the mystery. He found himself becoming more and more engrossed in the world of ancient magic and occult knowledge, and he knew that he was taking a risk.

But as he uncovered more and more fragments of the mystery, he began to feel a sense of exhilaration. He was getting closer, he could feel it. And he knew that once he had uncovered the truth, he would be able to unlock a power that few had ever known.

As the days passed, Dr. Raj began to notice a change in himself. He became more focused, more intense. He found himself speaking in whispers and muttering shlokas under his breath. He began to see things that he couldn't explain, and he knew that he was being pulled deeper and deeper into a world of ancient magic and occult knowledge.

And then, one day, as he was studying a particularly ancient text, he heard a knock at the door. He looked up to see the mysterious woman standing in the doorway, her expression grave.

"Dr. Raj," she said. "I need to speak with you. Something has happened."

Dr. Raj felt a shiver run down his spine. He could tell from her tone that something was very wrong.

"What is it?" he asked, rising from his seat.

"It's better if I show you," she said. "Come with me."

And with that, she turned and walked out of the room, Dr. Raj following close behind. He knew that he was about to enter a new level of danger, but he also knew that he had no other choice.

Together, they made their way through the winding streets of the city, until they arrived at a small, dimly-lit alleyway. The woman motioned for him to follow her, and they stepped into the darkness.

As they walked deeper into the alleyway, Dr. Raj began to feel a sense of unease building inside him. He knew that they were getting closer to the heart of the mystery, and he knew that whatever lay ahead would be dangerous.

And then, suddenly, the woman stopped in her tracks. She turned to face him, her eyes filled with a mixture of fear and determination.

"Dr. Raj," she said. "We're here."

Dr. Raj looked around, trying to make sense of their surroundings. The alleyway was narrow, and the walls on either side were covered in peeling paint and rusted metal. But as he looked closer, he noticed something odd about the way the walls seemed to be pulsing, as if they were alive.

"What is this place?" he asked, his voice barely above a whisper.

"It's a portal," the woman replied. "One that leads to the realm of the spirits."

Dr. Raj felt his heart skip a beat. He had read about portals before, but he had always believed them to be nothing more than myth. But now, standing in this narrow alleyway, he realized that he was about to enter a world that he had only ever read about in ancient texts.

The woman motioned for him to follow her, and they stepped closer to the pulsing wall. She reached out and placed her hand against the wall, and Dr. Raj watched as her fingers seemed to sink into the metal.

"Come," she said, turning to face him. "We have to hurry."

Dr. Raj took a deep breath and stepped forward, placing his own hand against the wall. He felt a jolt of electricity run through his body, and then suddenly he was falling, falling through a tunnel of darkness.

He landed on the other side with a thud, his eyes struggling to adjust to the bright light of the spirit realm. The woman was standing beside him, her expression grave.

"We have to be careful here," she said. "This is a place of great power, but also great danger. The spirits here are not like the ones in the mortal realm. They are old and powerful, and they do not take kindly to outsiders."

Dr. Raj nodded, his mind racing with excitement and fear. He had never felt so alive.

Together, they began to walk through the spirit realm, searching for something that the woman would not reveal. Dr. Raj saw things that he could not explain: trees made of fire, mountains that glowed with an inner light, and creatures that seemed to be made of smoke and shadows.

As they walked, Dr. Raj began to feel a sense of unease building inside him. He knew that they were getting closer to their goal, but he also knew that they were in great danger.

And then, suddenly, the woman stopped in her tracks. She turned to face him, her eyes filled with a mixture of fear and determination.

"Dr. Raj," she said. "We're here."

Dr. Raj's heart raced as he looked around, trying to understand what the woman meant by "we're here." The spirit realm was vast and seemingly endless, and he had no idea where they could possibly be.

"What do you mean, we're here?" he asked, his voice trembling slightly.

The woman's expression grew even more serious, and she took a deep breath before answering.

"I brought you here for a reason," she said. "There is something that you must do, something that only you can do."

Dr. Raj felt a sense of unease wash over him. He had a feeling that he was not going to like what she was about to say.

"You see, Dr. Raj," the woman continued, "the painting that you found, the one of Shreya, it is not just an ordinary painting. It holds great power, and there are those who would do anything to get their hands on it."

Dr. Raj felt his breath catch in his throat. He had suspected that there was something unusual about the painting, but he had never imagined that it could hold such power.

"What do I have to do with it?" he asked, his mind racing.

The woman looked at him with a mix of sadness and determination.

"You must protect it, Dr. Raj," she said. "Protect it at all costs. There are those who will stop at nothing to get their hands on it, and if they succeed, it could mean the end of everything."

Dr. Raj felt a sense of dread building inside him. He had never been much of a fighter, and he had no idea how he could possibly protect the painting from those who would seek to take it.

"But how?" he asked. "How can I possibly protect it?"

The woman's expression softened, and she placed a hand on his shoulder.

"That is for you to figure out, Dr. Raj," she said. "But I believe in you. You have a strength inside you that you have not yet tapped into. You must find that strength and use it to protect the painting."

Dr. Raj nodded, feeling a sense of determination building inside him. He knew that he had no choice but to protect the painting, no matter what the cost.

But as he turned to face the woman, he noticed something odd about her expression. There was a hint of sadness in her eyes, and he could sense that there was something she was not telling him.

"What is it?" he asked, his voice barely above a whisper.

The woman hesitated for a moment before answering.

"There is something else you must know," she said. "Something that I have been keeping from you."

Dr. Raj felt his heart race as he waited for her to continue.

"The woman who warned you about the painting, the one who wrote the letter, she was not just anyone," the woman said. "She was someone very important, someone who knew more about the painting than anyone else.

Dr. Raj felt a sense of confusion wash over him. He had assumed that the woman who had warned him was the same women who was in front of him telling him everything, but now it seemed that there was more to her than he had realized.

"Who was she?" he asked, his voice barely above a whisper.

The woman hesitated again, her eyes flickering with emotion.

"She was my sister," she said, her voice barely above a whisper.

# IV

# Searching for Answers about Shreya's Disappearance

Dr. Raj felt a jolt of shock run through him as he realized the connection between the woman before him and the mysterious women in the dormitory 207. He couldn't help but wonder what kind of relationship the two sisters had, and what secrets they shared.

"Your sister?" he repeated, feeling as though his mind was struggling to keep up with the rapid twists and turns of the story.

The woman nodded, a sad smile tugging at the corners of her lips.

"Yes," she said. "My sister and I were very close. We grew up together, and even as adults we remained inseparable. But there was something about Shreya that always set her on edge."

Dr. Raj felt a sense of unease as the woman began to speak, her voice low and filled with emotion.

"Shreya was a beautiful girl, inside and out," she said. "She was kind and gentle, and had a way of making everyone around her feel at ease. But she was also very naive. She trusted people easily, and sometimes that got her into trouble."

The woman paused for a moment, her eyes clouded with memories.

"Shreya fell in love with a man named Vikram," she continued. "He was charming and handsome, and at first, he seemed like the perfect match for her. But my sister was not convinced. She had a feeling that there was something off about him, something that she couldn't quite put her finger on."

Dr. Raj listened intently, feeling as though he was being pulled into the story.

"The painting," she said, "is a key to finding out what happened to Shreya. It was the last thing she received as a gift on before she disappeared. And I believe that it holds a clue, something that will help us find her and uncover the truth about what happened." Dr. Raj felt a surge of excitement mixed with a deep sense of foreboding. He knew that getting involved in this mystery could be dangerous, but he couldn't resist the pull of the woman's story. "I'll do everything I can to help," he said, his voice resolute. "We'll find out what happened to Shreya, and we'll make things right." The woman nodded, a look of gratitude on her face. "Thank you," she said. "I knew that I could count on you. But we must be careful. There are powerful forces at work here, and we don't know who we can trust." Dr. Raj nodded, feeling a sense of determination rising within him.

He knew that the road ahead would be difficult and filled with danger, but he was ready to face whatever challenges lay ahead. For the sake of Shreya, he was willing to risk everything.

"The painting," she said, her voice barely above a whisper. "It was Shreya's. Vikram had given it to her as a gift, as a way to symbolize his hold over her. She cherished it. But when she disappeared, the painting disappeared with her and now you found it somehow" Dr. Raj felt a sense of dread settle over him. He knew that he was getting closer to the truth, but he couldn't help but wonder what kind of danger he was putting himself in by pursuing this mystery. "I have to find her," he said, his voice firm with conviction. "I have to know what happened to Shreya, and more about that painting." The woman looked at him with a mix of fear and admiration. "I can't help you with that," she said. "But I can tell you this. If you keep looking, if you keep digging, you will find the truth. And the truth will set you free." With those words, the woman rose to her feet and disappeared into the night, leaving Dr. Raj alone with his thoughts. He knew that he had a difficult road ahead of him, filled with danger and uncertainty. But he also knew that he couldn't give up, not now. He had to find Shreya, and he had to solve this mystery, no matter what it took.

# V

# The Quest for Truth: Dr. Raj's Journey with Bharkandeshwar Baba to Confront the Dark Secrets of Their City

Dr. Raj felt a sense of unease as he drove to meet Bharkandeshwar Baba, the holy man who was said to have an incredible understanding of the spiritual world. He had heard stories about the baba's powers and felt nervous about meeting him, but he knew that he needed to keep the painting safe and that Baba might have some answers for him.

As he arrived at the ashram, Dr. Raj felt a sense of peace wash over him. The ashram was a beautiful place, surrounded by lush green forests and peaceful gardens. He was greeted by a group of disciples who led him to the baba's quarters.

The baba was an old man, with a long beard and a kind face. He welcomed Dr. Raj with a smile and invited him to sit down.

"I understand that you have a painting that you need to keep safe," the baba said, his voice deep and resonant.

Dr. Raj nodded, feeling a sense of relief that the baba already seemed to know what he needed help with.

"The painting is of great importance to me," he said. "It has a mysterious connection to a woman I am trying to find."

The baba nodded sagely. "I see. The painting has a powerful energy within it, and it must be kept safe from those who seek to use its power for their own purposes."

Dr. Raj listened intently as the baba spoke, feeling a sense of awe at the depth of his knowledge.

"You must keep the painting in a place that is sacred and protected," the baba continued. "I suggest that you find a temple or shrine, somewhere that is consecrated to the divine. There, the painting will be safe from harm."

Dr. Raj felt a sense of gratitude as the baba spoke, and he knew that he had found the answer he had been searching for. He thanked the holy man and left the ashram feeling lighter than he had in weeks.

Over the next few days, Dr. Raj searched for the perfect place to keep the painting. He visited several temples and shrines, but none of them felt quite right. Finally, he stumbled upon an old abandoned Temple in the heart of the city.

As he walked into the Temple, Dr. Raj felt a sense of peace wash over him. The Temple was silent and still, with shafts of sunlight streaming through the stained-glass windows. He knew that this was the perfect place to keep the painting.

With the help of some friends, he set up a small altar in the Temple, placing the painting at the center. He lit candles and incense, and as he sat in silence, he felt a powerful energy emanating from the painting.

Dr. Raj knew that the painting was safe now, and he felt a sense of relief wash over him. But he also knew that his journey was far from over. He still had so many questions about the woman in the painting, about her connection to the mysterious letter-writer, and about the dark secrets that lay hidden beneath the surface of his own city. He knew that he would have to continue his search, no matter where it took him.

And so, Dr. Raj continued his quest, seeking answers to the many mysteries that surrounded the painting and the woman in it. He scoured old archives, talked to historians and experts, and even travelled to remote villages and towns in search of clues. As he delved deeper into the mystery, Dr. Raj began to uncover a web of intrigue and deception that went far beyond what he had imagined. He learned of powerful forces at work, and of secret societies that operated in the shadows. Despite the danger and the obstacles, Dr. Raj was determined to uncover the truth. He worked tirelessly, following every lead, and piecing together the fragments of the puzzle, until finally, he found what he had been looking for. The truth was shocking, and it threatened to upend everything that Dr. Raj had ever believed. But he knew that he could not turn away from it. He had to face it head-on, no matter what the consequences. With a heavy heart, Dr. Raj took a deep breath and stepped into the unknown, ready to confront the dark secrets that lay hidden beneath the surface of his own city.

As the days passed, Dr. Raj sensed a growing tension in the air. He heard whispers of a battle between Bharkandeshwar Baba and the Soul of Vikram, a powerful and malevolent spirit that was said to be wreaking havoc in the city.

Dr. Raj had heard rumors that Vikram had made a deal with dark forces to gain immense power and was using it to terrorize the innocent. The baba, on the other hand, was known to possess incredible spiritual strength and was believed to be the only one who could defeat Vikram and put an end to his reign of terror.

One evening, Dr. Raj decided to visit the baba at his ashram to see if he could shed any light on the situation. When he arrived, he found the ashram in chaos. The disciples were frantically preparing for an imminent attack, and the baba himself was in deep meditation, preparing to face Vikram.

Dr. Raj watched in awe as the baba emerged from his trance and summoned all his spiritual strength. He began to chant mantras and perform ancient rituals, drawing upon the power of the divine.

Suddenly, the Soul of Vikram appeared in a cloud of smoke, his eyes glowing red with hatred. He laughed maniacally as he attacked the baba with bolts of dark energy, but the baba stood firm, deflecting the attacks with a shield of divine light.

The battle raged on for what felt like hours, the air crackling with energy. Dr. Raj watched in amazement as the baba called forth the power of the elements, summoning lightning and thunder to strike down Vikram.

But Vikram was not so easily defeated. He fought back with all his might, unleashing a barrage of dark magic that threatened to overwhelm the baba. Dr. Raj watched in horror as the two combatants circled each other, locked in a deadly struggle.

Finally, after what felt like an eternity, the baba emerged victorious. With a final burst of spiritual energy, he banished Vikram back to the realm of darkness from which he had come.

As the ashram erupted in cheers and celebrations, Dr. Raj felt a sense of awe and wonder. He had witnessed a battle between the forces of light and darkness, and he knew that he had seen something truly extraordinary.

As he left the ashram, he knew that his journey was far from over. There were still so many mysteries to uncover, so many secrets to unravel. But he also knew that he had the support of the baba and his disciples, and he felt a sense of renewed determination to continue his quest for the truth.

As Dr. Raj was recovering from the intense encounter between Bharkandeshwar Baba and the soul of Vikram, he couldn't help but wonder what other secrets lay hidden in the city. He knew that the baba had saved his life, and he felt a deep sense of gratitude towards him. But he also knew that the city was still in danger, and that there were other powerful forces at play.

Over the next few days, Dr. Raj tried to piece together everything he had learned. He revisited the abandoned temple where he had left the painting, and he felt a sense of calm and safety there. But he also knew that he could not let his guard down, not even for a moment.

One evening, as he was walking home from work, he heard a strange noise coming from a nearby alleyway. He hesitated for a moment, but then he felt a powerful urge to investigate. As he turned the corner, he saw a group of shadowy figures gathered around a small fire.

He recognized the symbols they were using, and he knew that they were performing a dark ritual. He watched in horror as they chanted and summoned a powerful force from the shadows.

Dr. Raj knew that he had to act fast. He had no weapons, no backup, and no plan. But he also knew that he could not let this evil go unchecked. He took a deep breath and stepped forward.

At first, the shadowy figures did not even notice him. They were too focused on the ritual. But as he approached, one of them turned and saw him. He shouted a warning, and the others turned to face him.

Dr. Raj felt a surge of fear, but he also felt a powerful energy welling up within him. He knew that he had to stop them, no matter what the cost.

He charged forward, using all his strength and speed. He threw punches and kicks, dodged their attacks, and fought with everything he had. But in vein.

# VI

# Lost Love: The Love Story of Shreya and Vikram

Dr. Raj woke up in a dark and unfamiliar place. He looked around and saw nothing but shadows surrounding him. He tried to move, but he realized that his body was paralyzed. Fear crept up his spine as he heard a sinister voice whisper in his ear, "Welcome to the past, Dr. Raj." Suddenly, a bright light appeared, and the shadows vanished. Dr. Raj found himself transported to a different time, a different place. He was standing in the middle of a lush garden, surrounded by fragrant flowers and chirping birds. He noticed a young couple sitting under a tree, holding hands and gazing into each other's eyes. The woman had a striking resemblance to the woman in the painting - Shreya.

As Dr. Raj approached them, he realized that the man was Vikram. He watched as they laughed and talked, oblivious to the world around them. They looked so happy and in love. Dr. Raj couldn't help but feel envious of their happiness. He wondered how such a beautiful love story had turned into a tragic one.

As he watched them, he saw how Vikram looked at Shreya with such adoration and love, and how she gazed back at him with the same intensity. They talked and laughed, enjoying each other's company and the beauty of their surroundings.

Dr. Raj was mesmerized by their love story, feeling as though he was witnessing something truly special. He saw how they would hold hands and take walks through the gardens, lost in their own little world. And he felt their connection as if it were his own.

As Dr. Raj watched the past unfold before him, he couldn't help but be drawn into the love story of Shreya and Vikram. He saw the two of them meet in college, both studying medicine and passionate about their work. They were both driven, ambitious and had a zest for life that drew them to each other.

Dr. Raj saw them laugh, study and spend countless hours together, discussing everything from their future plans to their favourite books. As he watched them, he could see the deep love and connection they shared, and he couldn't help but feel a twinge of sadness for what had happened.

As the memories unfolded, Dr. Raj saw how their love blossomed into a deep and powerful bond. He saw how they faced challenges together, supporting each other through the ups and downs of life. He saw the beautiful moments they shared, from long walks in the park to romantic dinners by candlelight.

Dr. Raj felt like he was living in their memories, experiencing their emotions and feeling the depth of their love. He saw how they stood by each other through thick and thin, never once losing faith in each other.

Shreya and Vikram spent every moment they could together. They explored the city, went to movies, and took long walks in the park. They talked about everything and nothing, and they never seemed to run out of things to say. Vikram had a way of making Shreya feel like the most important person in the world, and she had never been happier.

One day, as they sat on a bench in the park, Vikram took Shreya's hand and looked into her eyes. "Shreya," he said, his voice soft and serious. "I have to tell you something. I love you."

Shreya's heart skipped a beat as she looked at Vikram. She had known for a while that she loved him too, but hearing him say it out loud made her feel like she was flying. "I love you too, Vikram," she said, feeling her cheeks flush.

From that day on, they were inseparable. They talked about their dreams and their future together. Vikram was an artist, and he showed Shreya his paintings, which were filled with color and life. Shreya had always been interested in photography, and she took pictures of everything they saw together.

As the days passed, Shreya and Vikram grew closer and closer. They shared everything with each other, their hopes, and their fears. They knew that they were meant to be together, and nothing could ever tear them apart.

But fate had other plans for them. One day, Vikram received news that his father had passed away, leaving him with the responsibility of taking over the family business. Shreya saw the change in Vikram as he became more and more consumed by his work. He spent long hours at the office, and when he came home, he was too tired to spend time with her. Shreya tried to be understanding, but she couldn't help feeling neglected. She missed the long walks and the talks they used to have. She missed the way he used to look at her, as though she was the only thing that mattered. She knew that Vikram still loved her, but she couldn't help feeling like she was losing him. As time passed, their relationship began to suffer. They argued more, and the distance between them grew. Vikram became more distant, and Shreya felt like she was losing him. She tried to talk to him, to make him understand how she felt, but he didn't seem to listen.

One day, Shreya decided that she couldn't take it anymore. She packed her bags and left, feeling heartbroken and alone. Vikram tried to reach out to her, but she didn't want to listen. She felt like he had betrayed her, like he had chosen his work over her.

Dr. Raj watched the love story of Shreya and Vikram unfold before him, feeling the pain and heartache that they had gone through. He felt like he was living through their memories, experiencing their emotions as if they were his own.

Suddenly, he felt a jolt, and he was back in the present. He looked around, disoriented, and saw Bharkandeshwar baba standing in front of him, his eyes full of concern. "Are you okay?" the baba asked. Dr. Raj nodded, still feeling the weight of the past on his shoulders. "I saw their love story," he said, his voice filled with emotion. Bharkandeshwar baba nodded, understanding the pain that Dr. Raj had experienced. "Their love was powerful and beautiful," he said. "But sometimes, life gets in the way, and we lose sight of what's important." Dr. Raj nodded, feeling a sense of clarity wash over him. He realized that he had been so focused on finding a solution to his problem that he had lost sight of the things that mattered most. He knew that he needed to go back to the present and make things right. As he got up to leave, Bharkandeshwar baba gave him a small smile.

"Remember," he said. "Love is the most powerful force in the universe. It has the power to heal and to conquer all obstacles. Don't forget that." Dr. Raj nodded, feeling a newfound sense of hope. He knew that he had a lot of work to do, but he was ready to face the future, knowing that he had the power of love on his side.

# VII

# The Mysterious Map

Dr. Raj opened his eyes and found himself lying on a hospital bed, surrounded by medical equipment. He tried to sit up, but he felt weak and groggy. A nurse rushed to his side, and she told him that he had been found unconscious in the park, and someone had brought him to the hospital.

Dr. Raj's head was spinning as he tried to remember what had happened. He had a vague memory of being transported to a different time and place, but he couldn't make sense of it. As he lay in the hospital bed, Dr. Raj thought about Shreya and Vikram's love story. He wondered what had happened to them after they had separated. Had they found happiness with someone else, or had they always regretted their decision? He wanted to know more about them, to understand the depth of their love and the pain of their separation.

After he was discharged from the hospital, Dr. Raj decided to search for more information about Shreya and

Vikram. He went to the library and spent hours looking through old newspapers and archives, trying to find any information about them. Finally, he came across an article that mentioned Vikram's name. It was an interview with a famous artist, and he talked about how he had been inspired by the love of his life, Shreya. Dr. Raj's heart skipped a beat as he read the article. He had finally found a clue about what had happened to Shreya and Vikram. He continued to search for more information, and he found out that Vikram had become a successful businessman, but he had never stopped painting.

Shreya had become a photographer and had traveled the world, capturing its beauty through her lens. Dr. Raj felt a sense of relief knowing that they had both found success in their chosen fields, but he couldn't help wondering if they had ever found happiness with someone else.

As Dr. Raj continued his search for more information. Dr. Raj felt a sense of loss, knowing that he would never have the chance to meet him in person and hear more about his love story with Shreya. He wondered how Shreya had coped with the loss of her soulmate and if she had found happiness after all these years.

Dr. Raj decided to visit Vikram's art gallery to pay his respects and see if he could learn more about his life. As he walked through the gallery, he was amazed by the beauty and depth of Vikram's paintings. Each one was a masterpiece, and Dr. Raj could feel the passion and love that had gone into creating them. He introduced himself to the staff and asked to see any paintings that were related to Shreya. The staff member took him to a back room, and Dr. Raj saw a painting that took his breath away. It was a portrait of Shreya, her eyes filled with a mix of sadness and longing. Dr. Raj could feel the emotion that had gone into creating the painting, and he knew that Vikram had loved Shreya with all his heart. As he stood there, lost in thought, the staff member told him that there was a letter addressed from Vikram.

Dr. Raj's heart skipped a beat as he opened the envelope and read the letter. It was a heartfelt message from Vikram, about his love for Shreya and how much he had missed her since she had left. He talked about how he had found solace in his paintings and how each one was a tribute to their love. Dr. Raj felt tears welling up in his eyes as he read the letter. He could feel the pain and longing in Vikram's words, and he knew that their love story was one for the ages. He realized that sometimes, true love is not about being together forever but about cherishing the memories and the moments that you shared. As Dr. Raj left the gallery, he felt a sense of peace wash over him. He realized that even though Vikram and Shreya's love story had come to an end, it would live on through the beauty of Vikram's paintings and the memories that he had left behind.

Dr. Raj left the art gallery feeling grateful for the experience and the opportunity to learn more about Shreya and Vikram's love story. As he walked through the streets, he thought about how their story had touched his heart and how it would inspire others who heard it. He realized that sometimes, life takes unexpected turns, but it's up to us to find meaning and purpose in our experiences.

It was a night time. Rains were causing a Rattling sound. Dr. Raj was feeling some discomfort staying in his bed. He was feeling as if someone is calling him.

"Raaj, Raaaaaaaj, Raaaaaaaaaaaaaaaaaaaj". He wondered how come rains are making this sound. He got up and saw that envelope which he received from Art Gallery. It was a dreadful moment when he saw, what was written in an Envelope. It was a Map. Dr. Raj wore his slippers, took a raincoat and went out tracing that map. That map lead him to an abandoned building in Dark Jungle by the side of Woods. As he walked through the dense foliage, he could feel his heart pounding in his chest. As he approached the building, he noticed that the doors were slightly ajar, and there was a strange energy emanating from within. Dr. Raj took a deep breath and pushed the doors open, ready to face whatever lay ahead.

Inside the building, Dr. Raj was met with a strange sight. The room was dimly lit, and there were candles burning everywhere. Strange symbols adorned the walls, and there was a strong smell of incense in the air. As he walked further into the building, he heard strange whispers coming from the shadows. Dr. Raj felt a shiver run down his spine as he realized that he was not alone.

He continued to explore the building, searching for any clues that might lead him to the truth about Shreya and Vikram. As he walked down a long, narrow corridor, he noticed that the walls were covered in strange, glowing markings. He felt drawn towards them, and he placed his hand on the wall, feeling a strange energy coursing through his veins.

Suddenly, he heard a voice calling out to him from the darkness. "Dr. Raj," the voice whispered, "you have come to seek the truth about Shreya and Vikram." Dr. Raj froze in place, unsure of what to do. The voice continued, "Follow the path, and you will find what you are looking for." With that, the voice faded away, leaving Dr. Raj feeling both exhilarated and terrified.

He continued to follow the markings on the wall, feeling his heart beating faster with each step. The symbols seemed to be leading him towards a hidden doorway, and he pushed it open, ready to face whatever lay ahead. As he entered the room, he saw a figure standing in the corner, shrouded in darkness. "Who are you?" Dr. Raj asked, feeling a knot form in his stomach.

The figure stepped forward, and Dr. Raj gasped in shock. It was Shreya, looking just as beautiful as she had in the portrait. "I have been waiting for you, Dr. Raj," she said, her voice soft and soothing. "I know that you are searching for the truth about Vikram and me."

Dr. Raj felt his pulse quicken as he looked into her eyes. He felt a deep sense of connection to her, as if they had known each other for years. Shreya took his hand and led him to a small room in the corner of the building. Inside, there was a strange object that looked like a crystal ball. "This is the key to understanding our connection," Shreya said, gesturing towards the object.

Dr. Raj looked into the crystal ball.

# VIII

# Confronting Vikram's Malevolent Soul

Shreya's voice was trembling as she recounted the events that led to Vikram's tragic demise. "Gradually after separating from Vikram I used to feel lonely. I gradually realised that being with Vikram is the only thing I wanted to do in my life. I started googling how to be back with Vikram and I saw a post from Twin Sisters who used Black Magic to keep people under control. I went to them and told whole situation to them. And we started experimenting with black magic, trying to uncover its secrets. But something went terribly wrong. Vikram started behaving erratically, as if he were possessed by a malevolent force.

I immediately took him to hospital. You as a doctor were there when Vikram was brought in, his eyes glazed and his body writhing in agony. But you turned a blind eye, too wrapped up in you own desires to leave early. And now,

Vikram is dead.

But death had not claimed him completely. His soul had been twisted by the dark magic that had been unleashed upon him. It seethed with a fiery rage, seeking vengeance against those who had wronged him.

I thought that the twin sisters could control Vikram's soul, but she had been wrong. It was too powerful, too fierce. Twin Sisters however managed to weaken Vikram's soul by taking most of his mythical powers into that painting. And now his soul was after the painting that held the remnants of its power. The painting that had once been a thing of beauty, now radiated an ominous aura that chilled the bones."

At that point Dr. Raj realised that it was he himself who is the cause of all this. Had he not left early that day, Vikram could have been saved. He realised He was searching Evil outside when he was himself the root cause of that evil. He knew that the painting was a cursed object, one that could bring ruin to anyone who dared to possess it. And now, Vikram's soul was after it, seeking to regain its lost power.

As they stood in the dimly lit room, they could feel the air growing colder, the shadows creeping closer. And then they saw it – a flicker of light in the corner of their eyes, a sign that Vikram's soul was near. It was a spectre of rage and pain, a being of pure malevolence.

Dr. Raj felt a chill run down his spine as he realized that he was caught up in something far beyond his understanding. He had delved too deep into the unknown, and now he was paying the price. But he would not give up. He would find a way to stop Vikram's soul, to put an end to the curse that had been unleashed upon them.

The night stretched on, filled with fear and dread. But Dr. Raj and Shreya did not falter. They knew that they had to confront the darkness head-on, to face their fears and overcome them.

"Let's not waste a moment and meet Bharkandeshwar Baba". Dr. Raj nodded with an essence of Hope in his eyes. "I have seen Bharkandeshwar Baba defeating the soul of Vikram. That painting is safe with him and we also will be safe there!"

"There ain't any Bharkandeshwar Baba, you fool". Said the women Dr. Raj met in the Dormitory that day and one of the twin sister. She was sitting there listening to all the conversations between Shreya and Dr. Raj from other room and got horrified listening to that inauspicious name Bharkandeshwar Baba. "That Bharkandeshwar baba was no one but Vikram. That temple, that fight, that everything was all his maya or we can say illusions that he showed to you to take that painting.".

Dr. Raj's heart sank as he realized that he had been fooled. The woman's words echoed in his mind, filling him with a sense of dread. He had thought that there was hope, that they could find a way to defeat Vikram's vengeful spirit. But now he knew that he had been chasing a false hope, one that had been crafted by the very entity he sought to destroy. The Shreya and the first twin sister remained silent, their faces pale and drawn. They knew the true nature of Vikram's soul, and they knew the power that it possessed. They had been the ones who had unleashed it upon the world, and now they were helpless to stop it.

Dr. Raj felt a surge of anger rise within him. How could they have been so foolish, so naive? They had played with forces that they did not understand, and now they were paying the price. But he was not ready to give up yet. He would find a way to stop Vikram's soul, to put an end to this nightmare once and for all.

As they huddled together in the small room, the darkness outside seemed to grow thicker, as if it were alive and closing in on them. The air grew colder, and the sound of footsteps echoed through the halls. They knew that Vikram's soul was getting closer, that its wrath would soon be unleashed upon them. Dr. Raj searched the room frantically, his eyes falling upon the envelope from Vikram's art gallery that took him there. It had some glowing words "दवेः मम रक्षकः। सर्वेषां विघ्नानां तस्मै त्रायतो॥" means God is my saviour. He will save me from all problems.

Dr. Raj started reading that loud and clear followed by Shreya and the first Twin Sister. All three of them started reading that loud and clear.

Vikram's soul was vanquished.

The room grew silent, the air heavy with the weight of what had just happened. Dr. Raj looked around, his eyes resting on the envelope. It no longer glowed with an ominous light, and the air around it seemed to have cleared.

He knew that the danger had passed, that they had triumphed over the darkness. But the victory was bittersweet. They came too close to losing themselves. They were shaken to their core, realizing the extent of the damage they had caused.

However this was temporary. Vikram's soul was still out somewhere with all his powers back and will be attacking with much more force soon.

# IX

# The Search for the Missing Twin and the Revelation of Family Secrets

Dr. Raj realized that he had been given a sign. The words on the envelope were a message from a higher power, a reminder that he was not alone in this fight. He looked up at Shreya and the twin sisters, feeling a renewed sense of hope. "We have to find the other twin sister," First Sister said. "We have to bring her here so that we can stop this curse once and for all." “You have to find my twin sister” – The bewildered first sister said gasping. And Shreya needs to saved at all cost. They knew that the other sister was the key to ending this nightmare, but they also knew that finding her would not be easy.

Dr. Raj and the sister spent the next few days searching for the missing twin. They combed through every corner of the city, following every lead they could find. They talked to everyone who knew anything about the twins, piecing together a story of loss and betrayal.

Dr. Raj and the twin sisters were about to give up hope when they received a cryptic message from an unknown sender. It was a map, with a location marked in red. They knew that it was a trap, but they also knew that they had no other choice. They had to follow the map, to find the missing twin and put an end to this curse.

They arrived at the location marked on the map, a dilapidated building on the outskirts of the city. It was dark and deserted, the only sound the rustling of leaves in the wind. They cautiously made their way inside, their hearts pounding with fear. As they walked deeper into the building, they heard a faint whisper. It was a voice, barely audible, but they knew that it was the missing twin. They followed the voice, their steps quickening with each passing moment. And then they saw, a figure huddled in a corner, her eyes closed in prayer.

An old lady. Dr. Raj was taken aback when he saw the old lady. She looked familiar, like someone he had seen before. As he walked closer, he realized that she was his long-dead grandmother. He couldn't believe his eyes. He had heard stories about her from his mother, but he had never seen her in person. How was it possible that she was here, alive and well? The old lady opened her eyes slowly, and a smile spread across her wrinkled face when she saw Dr. Raj. "My dear grandson," she said, her voice hoarse but filled with love. "I knew you would come. I have been waiting for you." Dr. Raj was stunned. He couldn't understand what was happening. How was his grandmother alive? And what did she have to do with the curse that had befallen the twin sisters? Dr. Raj was speechless, as the old lady started to speak. She told him a story about his family's past, a story that had been kept hidden from him. She told him about his grandfather's infidelity, and how he had abandoned his family for another woman. She told him how she and her twin sister were born out of that betrayal.

Dr. Raj was shocked and saddened by the story. He couldn't believe that his family had been hiding such a big secret from him. But at the same time, he felt a sense of relief. He finally knew the truth about his family's past.

As the old lady finished her story, Dr. Raj asked her the question that had been weighing heavily on his mind since he entered the building. "Grandmother, what can I do to get over the soul of Vikram that is haunting me?" The old lady looked at him with understanding in her eyes. "You must seek forgiveness, my dear," she said. "Forgive yourself for what you did and seek forgiveness from those you hurt. Only then will you be able to let go of the past and move on." Dr. Raj nodded, feeling grateful for his grandmother's words of wisdom. He knew that seeking forgiveness would not be easy, but he was willing to do whatever it takes to rid himself of the haunting soul.

As Dr. Raj contemplated his grandmother's words, he remembered the twin sisters who were still waiting outside. He turned to the old lady and asked, "Grandmother, how did you found me and contacted me?"

The old lady smiled at him and said, "My dear, I have been here all along, watching over you and I was the one who gave you that envelope to save you that day. I have been waiting for the right moment to reveal myself to you. As for my soul, it is at peace now that I have been able to share the truth with you and help you find a way to rid yourself of Vikram's haunting presence."

Dr. Raj felt a sense of comfort knowing that his grandmother's soul was at peace. He thanked her for her guidance and bid her farewell, promising to visit her again soon. As he walked out of the dilapidated building, he saw first sister waiting for him, anxious to know if he had found the missing twin.

Dr. Raj smiled at her and said with a tears of joy in his eyes, "We have found the missing twin". It's time for us to put an end to this curse and move on with our lives." With renewed determination, the trio set off to break the curse once and for all.

# X

# Breaking the Curse: A Spooky Journey to Find Vikram's Soul.

Dr. Raj, Shreya, and the first sister had learned about a holy place that could help find Vikram's soul and break the curse that was plaguing them. They set out on their journey, not knowing what to expect. The holy place was located in a remote part of the country, deep in the mountains. It was said to be a place of great power, where the gods themselves resided.

As they made their way towards the holy place, the road grew narrow and treacherous. They drove through thick forests and rugged terrain, with the wind howling around them. It felt like they were being guided towards the holy place by an invisible force.

Finally, they arrived at the temple. It was an old, dilapidated building, surrounded by mist and fog. The air was heavy with the smell of incense, and the ground beneath their feet felt ancient and sacred. The temple was built on a hill, and they had to climb a long flight of stairs to reach it.

As they climbed the stairs, they heard strange whispers in their ears, and the wind grew colder. It felt like they were being watched by something unseen. The temple itself was a towering structure, with intricate carvings and statues of gods and goddesses.

As they entered the temple, they were greeted by the sight of numerous saints and monks praying and chanting. But as soon as they caught sight of the trio, the mood in the temple shifted. The saints and monks stopped chanting and started glaring at them with anger in their eyes. The trio realized that their presence was unwelcome, and they tried to leave, but it was too late. The saints and monks had already surrounded them, blocking their way out.

The first sister was terrified, but Dr. Raj and Shreya stood tall, determined to face whatever came their way. They explained their situation to the holy men, telling them how they came to find Vikram's Soul and ask for forgiveness. But the holy men were not convinced. They believed that Dr. Raj and his friends were responsible for the curse, and that they had brought a great misfortune upon themselves.

Dr. Raj tried to reason with the holy men, but it was no use. The saints and monks started chanting again, this time not to bless them but to curse them. Trio could feel the weight of the curse bearing down on them, and they knew that they had to act fast.

They searched the temple for anything that could help them, but it seemed like there was no hope. Just as they were about to give up, Dr. Raj noticed a small statue in a corner of the temple. It was a statue of Lord Shiva, the god of destruction and transformation. Dr. Raj realized that this could be the key to breaking the curse. He knelt down in front of the statue and started praying, asking Lord Shiva to help them.

As he prayed, he felt a surge of energy, and he knew that his prayers had been heard. He stood up and turned to the saints and monks who were still chanting, their voices growing louder with each passing moment. He held up his hand and shouted, "Stop!" To everyone's surprise, the chanting stopped, and there was silence in the temple.

Dr. Raj told them that they had come to seek forgiveness and break the curse, and that they were willing to do whatever it takes to make amends. The holy men listened to Dr. Raj's words, and they saw the sincerity in his eyes. Slowly, they started to lower their guard, and the atmosphere in the temple started to change.

Finally, one of the monks spoke up. "If you truly seek forgiveness and wish to break the curse, there is a way. But be warned, it is a spooky way, and not for the faint of heart." The trio nodded eagerly, willing to do whatever it takes.

The monk told them that to find Vikram's soul, they must perform a ritual. They must go to a nearby cave, deep in the mountains, and light a lamp. The lamp must be made of ghee, and it must be kept burning throughout the night. They must then meditate and focus their minds on Vikram's soul. If they were successful, they would see a vision of Vikram, and they would know what to do next.

But the monk warned them that the cave was said to be haunted by evil spirits, and that they must be careful. They must not let their guard down, and they must stick together at all times. The trio thanked the monk and set out towards the cave.

As they made their way towards the cave, the road grew even more treacherous. The terrain was rugged, and the path was narrow and winding. The wind howled around them, and the trees swayed ominously in the darkness. The trio's hearts were pounding with fear, and they knew that they were in for a spooky and perilous journey ahead.

As they approached the cave, they could feel a chill running down their spines. The cave was dark and foreboding, and it felt like the entrance to the underworld itself. The trio gathered their courage and stepped inside, holding their lamp of ghee tightly.

As they walked deeper into the cave, they could hear strange sounds echoing around them. It sounded like whispers and moans, and it seemed like the cave was alive with the sounds of unseen creatures. The trio tried to ignore the sounds and pressed on, but their nerves were frayed, and their hands were shaking.

Suddenly, they heard a loud hiss, and they saw a pair of glowing eyes staring at them from the darkness. They froze in terror, realizing that they were not alone in the cave. The eyes moved closer, revealing the form of a large snake. It was black as night and looked like it was ready to strike.

Dr. Raj and Shreya tried to back away, but the snake slithered forward, blocking their path. The first sister was paralyzed with fear, and she couldn't move. The snake coiled itself around Dr. Raj's leg, and he felt its cold scales against his skin.

They knew that they had to act fast. Shreya remembered something she had read about snakes, and she whispered to Dr. Raj, "Stay still. Don't move. It won't attack unless it feels threatened." Dr. Raj nodded, and they both stood still, not daring to move a muscle.

The snake stared at them for a moment and then slithered away, disappearing into the darkness. The trio breathed a sigh of relief and pressed on, their nerves on edge.

As they walked further into the cave, they could hear strange whispers growing louder. They sounded like multiple voices, all speaking at once, and it was hard to make out what they were saying. The trio tried to ignore the sounds, but they could feel their fear growing with each passing moment.

Suddenly, they heard a loud scream, and they saw a figure running towards them. It was a woman, her face twisted in terror, and she was screaming at the top of her lungs. She ran past them, disappearing into the darkness, and the trio could hear her screams echoing around the cave.

They tried to follow her, but the cave was too dark, and they could barely see anything. They stumbled around blindly, their hands outstretched, hoping to find their way. The whispers grew louder, and the sounds of unseen creatures seemed to be closing in on them.

Just when they thought that they would never find their way out, they saw a faint light in the distance.

Then, they saw a shadowy figure emerge from the darkness. It was the ghost of a soldier who had died in the Mahabharata, and he was surrounded by 6000 evil souls of soldiers who had died with him. The trio realized that this was the evil spirit that the saints and Monks in the temple had warned them about. The soldier started to advance towards them, his eyes filled with hatred and anger.

The trio stood their ground, knowing that they could not back down. Dr. Raj took a step forward and addressed the soldier. "We mean you no harm. We only seek to find Vikram's soul and break the curse that is plaguing us." The soldier laughed mockingly, "You dare you enter my domain and make demands to me? You will pay for your arrogance with your lives!" With that, the soldier charged at them, and the evil souls followed.

"Dr. Raj, you must start meditating and I will protect you and Shreya at all costs", said First Sister with glowing red eyes, purple face and long hairs. First Sister with all his powers of Black Magic made a pentagon of fire around Dr. Raj and Shreya to guard them and started fighting.

# XI

# Dr. Raj's Journey to Defeat Evil Spirits

As Dr. Raj started meditating and he found himself at a place. A place which was a realm of pure beauty and divine radiance, beyond the limits of human comprehension. It is a place where the air is perfumed with the sweet scent of blooming flowers and the soothing sound of celestial music can be heard at all times. The sky is a never-ending expanse of deep azure, dotted with golden stars that twinkle like precious jewels. There were shimmering waterfalls cascading down mountainsides, crystal clear lakes teeming with exotic and wondrous creatures, and lush gardens overflowing with fragrant flowers and succulent fruits. The colors are more vivid and intense than anything one can find on earth, and the air is imbued with a life-giving essence that rejuvenates the soul. He could very well see celestial fishes flying on the sky, their coats shining like diamonds, and dragons fly through the clouds, their scales glittering in the sunlight.

"Namaste Dr. Raj." Said a monk standing by his side.

Dr. Raj turned to face the monk, still marvelling at the stunning beauty of this realm. The monk had a serene expression on his face and exuded an aura of tranquillity that immediately put Dr. Raj at ease.

"Namaste," replied Dr. Raj. "I am amazed by the beauty of this place. Where are we?"

"This is a realm beyond the physical world, a place of pure consciousness and divine energy," said the monk. "Here, you can connect with the highest aspects of your being and tap into the infinite wisdom and power of the universe."

Dr. Raj felt a surge of energy and inspiration as the monk spoke. He knew that he was in the presence of a wise and enlightened being.

"I have come seeking your guidance, venerable one," said Dr. Raj. "I am facing a great challenge. Some evil spirits have attacked us in the cave and I am certain that first sister wont stand long against them."

The monk nodded, his eyes filled with compassion.

"I understand your plight, Dr. Raj," he said. "The forces of darkness are powerful and can be difficult to overcome. But fear not, for you have the power within you to defeat them."

Dr. Raj looked at the monk in surprise. "Me? But how? I am just a doctor."

The monk smiled. "Do not underestimate yourself, my friend. You have a pure heart and a noble spirit. These are the qualities that can conquer even the darkest of forces. But you must first learn to connect with your inner strength and cultivate your spiritual awareness."

Dr. Raj listened intently as the monk taught him various meditation techniques and spiritual practices. He felt a sense of peace and clarity wash over him as he absorbed the teachings.

"Remember, Dr. Raj," said the monk. "The battle against evil is not won through force or aggression, but through love and compassion. When you connect with the divine essence within yourself, you tap into an infinite source of power that can heal and transform even the most troubled souls."

Dr. Raj felt inspired and uplifted by the monk's words. He knew that he had found the key to defeating the evil spirits. With newfound confidence and determination, he bid farewell to the monk and returned to the physical world, ready to put his newfound wisdom into practice.

The condition of the First sister was dire. She was surrounded by a horde of evil spirits that were attacking her relentlessly. Her body was weak, and she was struggling to fend off the spirits with her limited strength. Her mind was clouded, and she couldn't think clearly, making it difficult for her to come up with a strategy to defeat the spirits. Her aura was dim, and she was losing her life force rapidly as the spirits continued to drain her energy. Despite her best efforts, she was slowly losing the battle and was on the verge of being consumed by the spirits.

Shreya's heart was pounding in her chest, and she was trembling with fear. She had never felt so helpless and vulnerable before. The spirits seemed the spot with their dark magic. Shreya began to panic, and tears welled up in her eyes as she realized that she was completely helpless.

The spirits began to circle around her, their mocking laughter echoing through the cave. Shreya could feel their cold fingers brushing against her skin, and she could hear their whispers in her ear. They seemed to be taunting her, telling her that she was weak and that she would never be able to defeat them.

Shreya knew that she needed help, but she didn't know where to turn. She was alone, and the spirits seemed to be growing stronger with each passing moment. She closed her eyes and began to pray, hoping that someone or something would come to her rescue.

In that moment, she felt a surge of warmth and light spread through her body. It was as if a powerful force was pushing back against the evil spirits, and she could feel their grip on her weakening. Shreya opened her eyes and saw a bright light shining in front of her. It was Dr. Raj, and he had come to save her from the spirits.

With his guidance and support, Shreya was able to summon her inner strength and overcome the evil spirits. She learned to face her fears and trust in her own abilities, and she emerged from the experience stronger and more confident than ever before.

"You people are strong and we are not here to fight, rather we are here to help you all and bring you all to peace", said Dr. Raj. "Tell me, what desire of yours remain unfulfilled and preventing you all to rest in peace?".

The evil spirits of Mahabharata looked at Dr. Raj with suspicion, but they could feel his power and knew that he spoke the truth. They hesitated for a moment before finally speaking.

"We are the spirits of the warriors who killed Abhimanyu in the Chakravyuha battle formation. Our desire is to tell the truth about how we killed him and to seek forgiveness for our actions," said the leader of the spirits.

Dr. Raj listened patiently as they recounted the events of that fateful day. They told him how they had attacked Abhimanyu when he was unarmed and how they had taken advantage of his youthful inexperience to overpower him. They spoke of their regret and their longing for redemption.

Dr. Raj could sense the sincerity in their words, and he knew that they were ready to move on. He took a deep breath and spoke softly to them. "I understand your pain and regret, but you must also understand that what you did was wrong. Abhimanyu was a brave and honorable warrior, and he did not deserve to die in such a way. You must seek forgiveness for your actions and do what you can to make amends. Only then can you find peace."

"pārtha na eva iha nāmutra vinaśas tasya vidyate na hi kalyāṇa-kṛt kaścid durgatim tāta gacchati – meaning Lord Krishna says to Arjuna, "O Partha, one who engages in devotional service to Me does not fall down in any circumstance. Having obtained the human birth, which is the highest form of life, one must endeavor to achieve Self-realization, and that can be done by surrendering unto Me. Because I am omnipresent, I am present everywhere at all times.". Lord Krishna was always here watching you and now its high time you should seek forgiveness.

The spirits listened intently to Dr. Raj's words, and as he spoke, they could feel a weight lifting from their souls. They knew that they had been forgiven, and they were grateful for the chance to make things right. With a final nod to Dr. Raj, the spirits disappeared, their voices echoing through the cave as they moved on to the next world. Shreya and Dr. Raj stood in silence for a moment, feeling the power of the spirits' release. "Well done, Dr. Raj," said Shreya, a smile spreading across her face. "You truly are a master of your craft." Dr. Raj smiled back at her, knowing that he had made a difference in the lives of those spirits and in the world. He knew that there was still much work to be done, but he was ready for whatever challenges lay ahead.

As Dr. Raj approached the first sister, he noticed that her condition was worsening. Her body was wracked with convulsions, and she was struggling to breathe. He knew that he had to act fast if he wanted to save her.

He looked around the cave, hoping to find some other source of medicine, but all he could see were snakes and poisonous plants. He knew that he had to act quickly if he wanted to save the first sister's life.

Suddenly, he had an idea. He remembered a plant that grew in the nearby forest that had powerful healing properties. He had used it before to treat similar problems, and he knew that it could help the first sister.

Dr. Raj turned to Shreya and said, "I need to go out and get a plant that will help treat the first sister's problems. Can you hold off the condition of First Sister while I'm gone?"

Shreya nodded bravelyTop of Form

Dr. Raj smiled gratefully and headed out of the cave. He made his way through the dark forest, his heart pounding in his chest. He knew that he was taking a risk, but he also knew that he had to do everything in his power to save the first sister's life.

Finally, he found the plant he was looking for and quickly gathered a handful of leaves. He made his way back to the cave, dodging the snakes along the way.

When he arrived, he immediately set to work, grinding the leaves into a fine powder and mixing it with water to create a paste. He applied the paste to the first sister's wound and waited anxiously to see if it would work.

To his relief, the first sister's condition began to improve almost immediately. Her convulsions subsided, and her breathing became more regular. Dr. Raj knew that the plant had worked its magic once again.

Shreya looked at him in amazement. "How did you know about that plant?" she asked.

Dr. Raj smiled. "I have spent many years studying the medicinal properties of plants and herbs. It's amazing what you can learn when you take the time to listen to the natural world."

Shreya nodded, impressed by Dr. Raj's knowledge and skill. Together, they tended to the first sister, watching over her as she slowly regained her strength.

# XII

# The Eternal Love and Unity of Shreya and Vikram: A Journey Through Forgiveness, Release, and Beyond.

Dr. Raj, Shreya, and the First Sister were shocked to hear a voice coming from the bright light in front of them. As they approached the light, they saw the outline of a figure, slowly becoming more visible. It was the soul of Vikram.

Shreya fell to her knees, tears streaming down her face, "Vikram, is that really you?" she cried.

"Yes, my love, it is me," replied Vikram's soul,

The trio gathered around the bright light, and Vikram's soul explained to them that he had been trapped in this mortal Realm, unable to move on to the next world because of the guilt he felt about his past mistakes

"I know that I hurt you, Shreya," Vikram's soul said, "and for that, I am truly sorry. I have been carrying this guilt with me, and it has been preventing me from finding peace. But I have been shown a way to make amends, and that is why I am here."

Vikram's soul then led the trio in a powerful meditation, guiding them through a process of forgiveness and release. They each connected with their own inner strength and love, and as they did so, they felt the presence of the divine surrounding them.

Dr. Raj felt a surge of energy flow through him, and his mind became clear and focused. The First Sister's aura began to glow brighter, and she was filled with a sense of renewal and strength. Shreya felt a sense of healing, as if a weight had been lifted off her shoulders.

However happiness didn't lasted long as they were suddenly attacked by a snake demon, accompanied by a thousand hissing snakes. Dr. Raj, Shreya, and the First Sister were caught off guard, and they realized that they were no match for the powerful creature.

But just as they thought all was lost, the soul of Vikram appeared in his ethereal form glowing with a bright light.

Vikram's soul then stood between the trio and the snake demon, and with a wave of his hand, he banished the creature back to its realm. The trio watched in awe as the snake demon disappeared in a flash of light.

Dr. Raj and the First Sister were horrified as they watched the thousand snakes attack Shreya. They tried to fight them off but it was too late. Shreya fell to the ground, her body motionless.

As they mourned her passing, the bright light returned, and the soul of Vikram appeared before them. He looked at Shreya's lifeless body and then turned to the two survivors.

"I am sorry that I couldn't save her," said Vikram's soul. "But I promise you that I will take care of her in the realm of spirits. She will be at peace with me."

Dr. Raj and the First Sister watched as Vikram's soul enveloped Shreya's body in a warm, loving light. Her body slowly disappeared, and they knew that her soul was now reunited with Vikram's forever.

"I am grateful for everything you have done for us," said Dr. Raj. "You have helped us find forgiveness and release."

"Thank you," added the First Sister. "We will never forget what you have done for us."

Vikram's soul smiled at them and then slowly began to fade away.

"Remember, my friends," he said as he disappeared, "love is eternal. It lives on forever."

As Shreya's soul floated up towards the bright light, she felt a sense of peace wash over her. She had been reunited with her beloved Vikram, and she knew that they would be together forever.

Vikram's soul embraced her, and they looked into each other's eyes, feeling an intense love and connection that transcended time and space.

"I've missed you so much," said Shreya, tears streaming down her face.

"I've missed you too, my love," replied Vikram's soul,

Shreya felt a deep sense of gratitude towards Vikram's soul. He had been her anchor in life, and now he was her guide in death. Together, they floated towards the light, their souls merging into one.

As they entered the light, they felt a sense of unity and oneness with the universe. They were no longer separate beings, but a part of something greater than themselves. They had transcended the limitations of their physical bodies and were now free to explore the mysteries of the universe.

Shreya looked around her in wonder, taking in the beauty of the infinite expanse of space. She saw stars, galaxies, and nebulae swirling around her, their colors and patterns shifting and changing in an endless dance.

Vikram's soul took her hand, and they floated together towards a distant star. As they approached it, they saw that it was surrounded by a shimmering aura of light, and as they entered the aura, they felt a sense of warmth and love wash over them.

"This is our home now," said Vikram's soul, "a place where we can be together forever. A place of peace and joy, where we can explore the wonders of the universe and create new worlds of our own."

Shreya smiled, feeling a sense of excitement and wonder. She had never felt more alive, even though she was no longer in her physical body.

"Thank you for everything," she said, looking at Vikram's soul, "I couldn't have done it without you."

Vikram's soul smiled back at her, "We did it together, my love. And now, we'll be together forever."

Dr. Raj and the First Sister left the cave with heavy hearts, but they knew that Shreya was at peace, reunited with her beloved Vikram. As they emerged into the bright sunlight, they saw that the world had changed. The colors were brighter, the air was sweeter, and they felt a sense of peace that they had never experienced before.

When Dr. Raj reached home he saw an old looking envelope. He opened that envelope. It was written

*Dear Dr. Raj,*

*I hope this letter finds you well. I am writing to inform you that our dear departed Shreya and Vikram are happy in the realm of spirits. Though it has been hard for us to come to terms with their passing, it gives us peace to know that they are no longer suffering and are in a better place.*

*Hope you realize that love and forgiveness can transform any evil spirit into a good and divine spirit. It is our human nature to hold onto grudges and anger towards those who have wronged us, but we must remember that forgiveness is a powerful tool in breaking the cycle of negativity and transforming it into positivity. Shreya and Vikram were two individuals who lived their lives with love and kindness towards others, and it is only fitting that they have found peace in the realm of spirits. They always believed in the power of forgiveness and never held onto any grudges, no matter how hurt they may have felt.*

*As we continue to mourn their loss, we can honor their memory by practicing forgiveness and love towards one another. We can transform any negative energy into positive energy and live our lives in a way that reflects the goodness of their spirits.*

*Thank you for your support during this difficult time.*

*Sincerely,*

*You can call me Women who called you in the dormitory 207, Staff who gave you the envelope, Your great grandmother, The monk you found meditating in the cave, or Second Sister.*

Dr. Raj couldn't hold his tears reading that. He knew that he had been forever changed by their encounter with Shreya and the soul of Vikram. And he knew that he would carry there message of love and forgiveness with them always.

# EPILOGUE

With those words, Second Sister vanished into the forest, leaving me with a sense of wonder and possibility. I knew that I had been given a great gift, and I vowed to use it to help others and make a difference in the world.

Next day was my first class and I was nervous about what was to come. I walked into the classroom, and there was Dr. Raj, standing at the front of the room, waiting for us. As soon as he began to speak, I knew that this was going to be an extraordinary experience.

Dr. Raj spoke to us about the importance of love and compassion in the practice of medicine. He told us that being a doctor was not just about diagnosing and treating illnesses; it was about caring for people and helping them heal both physically and emotionally.

He emphasized the importance of listening to our patients and treating them with respect and kindness. He explained that when we treat our patients with love and forgiveness, we create an environment of trust and comfort.

Dr. Raj also shared personal anecdotes from his own life where he had encountered difficult patients and how he managed to handle those situations with love and compassion. He told us that every patient is unique and that we must approach each one with an open heart and mind.

As the class ended, Dr. Raj reminded us that as doctors, we hold a great responsibility to care for our patients with empathy and understanding. He encouraged us to continue to learn and grow throughout our medical education and to always remember the importance of love and forgiveness in our practice.

That first class with Dr. Raj was a transformative experience for me. I realized that being a doctor is not just about having medical skills and knowledge but also about having the right attitude and mindset. I left that classroom feeling inspired and motivated to become a doctor who truly cares for and supports their patients.

9 798889 866657

Printed by Libri Plureos GmbH in Hamburg, Germany